To John

Grandma

Rose and Samuel
Lagercrantz

OF GERANIUM
STREET

pictures by Eva Eriksson
adapted from the Swedish by Jack Prelutsky

Greenwillow Books, New York

Library of Congress Cataloging-in-Publication Data
Lagercrantz, Rose, (date)
Brave little Pete of Geranium Street.
Translation of: Att man kan bli stark del 63.
Summary: When he finally gets the cake he
believes will make him strong, Pete becomes
brave enough to face two bullies.
[1. Courage—Fiction.   2. Stories in rhyme]
I. Lagercrantz, Samuel.   II. Eriksson, Eva, ill.
III. Title.
PZ8.3.L216Br 1987   [E]   85-30197
ISBN 0-688-06178-8
ISBN 0-688-06181-8 (lib. bdg.)

This is the story of brave little Pete
Who lived in a house on Geranium Street
With his mother and father, one round and one slim,
His sister Rebecca, his big brother Jim,
His grandma who baked things and helped make him laugh,
His pet plastic fish, and his old stuffed giraffe.

He wished that he lived in a place filled with noise
Instead of a house much too quiet for boys.

In fact, it appeared if it weren't for Pete
Life would often be dull on Geranium Street.

One day in the street, back when Pete was just four,
And wishing that he wasn't four anymore,

Two big boys came by, and with screeches and roars,
They frightened him so, that he ran back indoors.

He raced through the house,
Banging into his mother,
He tripped on his father,
His sister, and brother.

He ran up, he ran down,
He ran out, he ran in,
He tripped once again,
And got stuck with a pin.
"Little Pete," said Rebecca,
"You're really too thin.

Now hear my advice
And you cannot go wrong—
Little Pete, you must eat,
If you eat, you'll be strong,
And you'll thump those big boys.
Now go eat, run along."

Pete thought and thought, then thought some more
Of what his sister said.
He thought until a tiny light
Blinked on inside his head.

"A magic cake is what I need,
 A purple one ... and red."
 He begged his mother, who replied,
"I'm busy—have some bread."

By now Pete was tired,
Just barely awake,
But he went to his father
And asked for that cake.

"We could make it right now,
I'd be strong, I'd be brave,
I could teach those bad boys
That they'd better behave.

"We could make it with herring, five leaves, and a flea,
We could put in potatoes and snake.
Six lions could help us, or maybe just three,
For lions can stir and can bake.
I would soon be so strong I could juggle a tree
If I just had a piece of that cake.

"But boxers and wrestlers who happen along,
And soldiers and bears on the road,
Should not try my cake, they're already so strong,
It would probably make them explode.

And bullies who try it will stumble and fall,
One taste and they'll hardly be able to crawl.

"But if you're weak, just have a bite,
And you'll grow muscles overnight."

"That seems quite grand," his father said,
"But now it's late, and time for bed."

"Don't make me go to bed," Pete cried
Into his parents' ears.
They picked him up and tucked him in,
And kissed away his tears,
Then tiptoed softly out of sight,
And left him there to sleep all night.

But Pete couldn't sleep, for his two special toys
Were not where he'd left them that day.
He hopped out of bed, making almost no noise . . .
Where were they . . . had they run away?

He searched till he found them,
Safe under his bed,
And he slept with them both
Cuddled close by his head.

Pete awoke the next day just as morning began,
With a smile on his face, and an excellent plan.
"I'll pretend to be sick...I will wobble and fall,
And my parents will give me that cake after all."

So he tumbled and fell,
And he kicked and he screamed,
But nobody noticed,
At least, so it seemed.

Pete hurried outside, but the big boys were there,
They teased him and tripped him and pulled on his hair.
He ran to the kitchen, his face wet with tears,
His sister said, "Hah! Bang their heads! Box their ears!"

That evening he stared at his supper,
There were foods that he never could stand,
He was happy when Grandma came over
With a brightly wrapped box in her hand.

"Little Pete!" she exclaimed as she stepped in the door,
"Here's the cake you've been waiting so patiently for,
But you know, it will only do wonders for you
If you finish your fish, and your vegetables, too."

Pete ate some fish and spinach,
They weren't fun to chew,
Then tasting just a bit of cake
He yelled, "I'll show those two!"
He grabbed the cake and ran outside,
"They're going to get it now," he cried.

His family was startled, they shouted, "Oh my!
Just what is he going to do?"
Little Pete soon forgot, for a snail happened by,
Right there in the street, near his shoe.

He sat playing games with snail for awhile,
It tickled his fingers and helped make him smile,
But when those two bullies sneaked closely behind,
He remembered the plan that he'd had in his mind.

He hoisted the cake, and he yelled, "Have a taste!
It is made out of terrible things."
"Oh no!" cried the boys, away the two raced.
Pete chased them as though he had wings.
"Go away!" they both shrieked, but ignoring their squeals,
Little Pete ran behind, staying right on their heels.

They ran till one stumbled and fell with a plop.
"Get ready!" yelled Pete, but the boy pleaded, "Stop!"
"Here it comes!" Pete exclaimed, but the boy, turning green,
 Shouted, "Put down that cake, and we'll stop being mean."
"Do you promise?" Pete asked, and they both shouted "Yes!"
 So Pete swallowed that cake in a minute or less.

"You're a very brave boy, little Pete," gasped the two,
"To chase after us...we're much bigger than you,
And since you're so brave, you're our friend from this day,
We won't ever tease you or chase you away."

Pete became their best friend, and each day until dark,
They played in the street and they played in the park,
The two bigger boys did their best to behave,
And they never teased Pete, for they knew he was brave.

Pete grew to be five and he grew to be ten,
He grew to be brave as the bravest of men.
He grew and he grew, till today he's all grown,
With two little children of his very own,
And he tells them sometimes in the park or the street
Of the days when their father was brave little Pete.

ROSE LAGERCRANTZ is a well-known author in her native Sweden with many books to her credit. She was awarded the Astrid Lindgren prize in 1979.
SAMUEL LAGERCRANTZ is the son of Rose Lagercrantz.

EVA ERIKSSON is familiar to young readers as the illustrator of **The Wild Baby** and **The Wild Baby Goes to Sea,** both written by Barbro Lindgren and adapted from the Swedish by Jack Prelutsky. She is also the illustrator of the popular toddler series about Sam.

JACK PRELUTSKY has written more than 20 books, including **The New Kid on the Block, The Queen of Eene, The Snopp on the Sidewalk,** and **Nightmares,** all ALA Notable Books, and many beloved holiday Read-alone books. Born and raised in New York, he and his wife now live in Albuquerque, New Mexico.